# LILLAN

# Gunilla B. Norris

# LILLAN

ILLUSTRATED BY NANCIE SWANBERG

Atheneum    New York

1968

Copyright © 1968 by Gunilla B. Norris
All rights reserved
Library of Congress catalog card number 68-18455
Published simultaneously in Canada by
McClelland & Stewart Ltd.
Manufactured in the United States of America
Printed by The Murray Printing Company,
Forge Village, Massachusetts
Bound by H. Wolff, New York
First Edition

Fondly for
ANNE HUSTON

# LILLAN

# 1

Lillan looked at her mother in disbelief.

"You're not going to rent the living room!" she cried.

Her mother nodded seriously and the now familiar lines of determination turned her mouth downwards.

"Yes, and the library."

"But they are the best rooms," cried Lillan. She loved the furniture. She loved to touch the smooth carved wood of the Louis the Fourteenth sofa and to gaze at the heavy tapestry on the big wall.

"They are the best rooms, and that is the reason we can rent them."

"But where will we go?" Lillan felt tears coming. Too much had happened. It wasn't fair.

*3*

Her mother was so different now that Papa had left them. Those lines in her face were there so often. Why couldn't things go on the same always?

Her mother laughed suddenly. "Oh Lillan, it isn't the end of the world. We'll live in the kitchen and the bedroom. And you can have the little spare room to yourself."

Lillan looked at her mother. She had laughed. But it wasn't a happy laugh. Her eyes were serious and worried as they had been for over a year.

Why had Papa done this to them? He was always so gay, always filled with gossip and laughter. But there were those awful times before she and her mother had gone to live with Morfar. Lillan had heard them quarrel in the night. Papa had said awful things and Mama had gone hard and her mouth went downwards. Always in the mornings Papa would be away and Mama had red and puffy eyes.

"Why did Papa leave?" Lillan asked the question again.

Her mother sighed and went to the stove to pour a cup of coffee. The kitchen seemed dark since the window faced north towards Mälaren, Statshuset and the old town of Stockholm.

*4*

"Why did he?" asked Lillan again.

"Because he didn't love me anymore," said Mama softly and sat down. "I've told you before, dear."

Lillan watched her hand trace the patterns on the red and white oilcloth on the table. Lillan bit her lip. How could you stop loving somebody? You couldn't just go, could you? It wasn't fair. She couldn't understand.

"Was he mad?" she demanded. "What did you do?"

"Lillan, it's over. I can't explain. Your father left when we went to Morfar's house and that is all. We have to do the best we can."

Again Lillan felt that awful feeling of not understanding, of being left out of something important, something she wanted to know.

"Why can't you tell me?"

"Darling, you are only ten. These things are too big to understand," said her mother gently.

"They aren't too big," answered Lillan determinedly. Why did grown-ups suppose you couldn't understand? Wasn't it better to know?

Lillan remembered the last time Papa had been with them. They had been on a trip. Mama had been worried about the money Papa had been spending. They had gone to lovely restaurants. Mama had gotten all worried.

"We can't afford this!" she said again and again. And Papa had laughed at her and then they had quarreled. Papa drank some whiskey, and to make Mama angrier, he had given Lillan some.

Mama had cried and said he didn't love her anymore, and then Papa said that was true. He took them to Morfar's house and left. After that . . . Lillan closed her eyes. That year with Morfar had been strange, sort of like a big exception of time, the way you wrote a parenthesis in a sentence.

"Let's not sit here and get long-nosed," said Mama. Her voice sounded suddenly bright but not quite real. Lillan looked at her a long time. There was something she wanted to ask. Something she wanted to know.

"Mama, did you stop loving Papa, too?"

Her mother turned away and busied herself with the cleaning pail.

"Did you?" insisted Lillan.

Her mother turned slowly away from the sink and looked at her. "Yes, Lillan, I did. It's all over and we must begin again."

Despite herself, Lillan shivered. She didn't want to ask anything more.

"Come on, we'll have to work hard," said Mama. "We'll clean the living room and the library. We'll have to make some kind of closet. Here's a dust rag. Will you dust the living room while I clean out the library desk?"

Lillan was glad of something to do. She took the rag and went into the bright large room. She sat on the red velvety sofa and traced the carved arms with her finger. The oriental rug gleamed with its bright colors on the floor. She had spun around and around on it as a little child until the whole room whirled about her. She had loved that game. And Papa had always laughed at her.

"Lillan, you'll be sick."

But she never was sick. The tapestry could go by in a whirlwind and the Dutch oil painting with the man with the long hair would smile down at her.

They hadn't worried then. They could afford things. Lillan remembered bowlfuls of blood oranges from Italy and Papa peeling them from top to bottom without any of the peel breaking. She remembered making egg toddies. They'd beat an egg yolk in a cup with lots of sugar. You'd beat and beat and beat until big bubbles came and the egg yolk turned white and

7

the sugar melted. Lillan remembered beating for hours to make it last longer.

That was all before there was war rationing and before Papa acted funny as if he didn't care how much he spent, as if he wanted everything to go wrong.

Lillan sighed and began to dust. Mama had taken all of Papa's little things and put them in a box: his silver cigarette case and his little music box. The room was empty of him now and it had been a long time. Mama had let the apartment to another family for a year while they had lived at Morfar's house. That is when she took everything away.

Then they had lived Morfar's life mostly, having little cups of tea and not talking about things that hurt or really mattered. Lillan had started school, and they had all gone on as if everything was all right. Until Mama got a paper that said she and Papa were not married anymore, that they were divorced.

That's when they had moved back to Stockholm in the late summer so that Mama could find work. Now Mama said they had to start over.

Lillan dusted the legs of the sofa gently. She would miss sitting there. She went over to the

tapestry. It always smelled of dust. Mama had said that Papa had bought it when they were first married. It was a joke. They needed a bed and furniture, but instead they had a tapestry. Lillan smiled and then her lips drew together. Did Mama stop loving Papa because he had been like that—getting tapestries and going to fancy restaurants when there were important things that were needed?

Lillan looked at the tapestry. There were moth holes in it. Peep holes really because you could play hide and seek behind the tapestry and still see everything. She had played with Papa.

"Where's Ingalill?" he would call and went to hunt for her. Of course, she knew that he knew where she was. And she could see through the peep holes. He'd act worried.

"Ingalill. My little girl is lost. My little one— Lillan—." That is how her nickname came . . . Lillan.

She stood there and she began to cry. Why did Mama want to rent this room? How could she do it? But Lillan knew why. She didn't love Papa anymore. He didn't love them. So you cleaned everything up and let someone else use it.

The tears came down hot and stingy and she couldn't see the tapestry or the sofa or the Dutch man on the wall with the long hair. What would happen if . . . if . . . Mama stopped loving . . .?

"Lillan," Mama stood in the doorway.

Lillan turned away. She didn't want her mother to see her crying. She bent down and began dusting the coffee table quickly.

"Lillan." Her mother came over to her and caught her up in her arms. "Lillan, don't cry."

She wriggled loose and turned her back.

"Darling, I am as sorry as you to let this room, but we need the money. We have to do it. School is starting next week. You need shoes and books. You'll need a coat when it grows colder. Please, darling, try to understand."

Lillan bit her lips and didn't answer.

"Sometimes you have to give things up. Sometimes you even have to give up loving someone. Papa has gone off to South America. He isn't with us anymore and he won't be. We just have to begin again."

Slowly her mother rose. "I think we need a little lunch now," she said and went to the kitchen.

## 2

They spent the week cleaning. Mama did
most of the work, and Lillan helped when she
could. But mostly she watched as things were
moved from their rightful place. At night Mama
was too tired to read or play flower lotto or even
talk. Lillan felt lonely, but she couldn't say anything. She didn't dare. Her mother wore that
look of determination, so Lillan kept silent as
Mama moved her things from the library, which
had been used for a bedroom. The desk was
empty. The favorite books were removed. The
curtains were starched and cleaned. It had a
lonely feeling about it. But the living room was
worse. Lillan didn't even want to go in there
anymore. Ever since Mama nailed up a shelf in
a corner with a curtain hanging from it. That

was the closet. The rooms were all ready now to be let by someone.

"Lillan, when the tenant comes you will be quiet, won't you?" said Mama absently one day. "We'll not be alone anymore. You'll have to close the front door quietly and come into our part of the apartment."

Lillan listened but didn't really hear. Her mother was saying all this because someone was coming to look at the rooms. She had heard the excitement in Mama's voice earlier on the telephone.

Now it was lunch time and Mama made them some oatmeal. She set the bowls down on the oilcloth and there was a pleased flush about her. It felt as if her mother hardly knew she was there.

Lillan looked down at the hot cereal. "Horrid porridge" is what Papa called it. She didn't touch it.

"If only she'll take them," said Mama dreamily. "Then we'll be able to make it fine this winter. We must hope she likes the rooms. Oh, Lillan," her mother turned to her, "I do hope it works out well."

It seemed to Lillan that was the first time her mother had looked at her all week.

"Aren't you hungry?" asked Mama.

"It's horrid porridge," mumbled Lillan.

"Oh Lillan, it is not. It sticks to your ribs. Just because your father turned his nose up at it is no reason for you to. We can't have chateaubriand and mushroom omelet. We can't afford it. You know how expensive everything is at the store. Besides, there isn't much to choose from now after the war."

Lillan blushed. Her mother always scolded like that, by telling you what you knew already. Lillan ate the oatmeal reluctantly. They had had oatmeal so often, and gruel with prunes and fish pudding that tasted like cardboard, and salt herring. There was never an end to the things that tasted salty or lumpy.

"Maybe we can have something good," said Mama softening, "if the lady takes the rooms. And then when school begins I can work."

Lillan looked at her mother as she wiped the kitchen table. She was so brisk, so busy. She didn't have time for Lillan.

Then the front doorbell rang. Mama looked up with anticipation. She smoothed her hair. "Hold your thumb for luck," she said and was out in the hall in a moment.

Lillan rose. She didn't want to see the lady

*14*

who was coming. She didn't want to hear her mother saying what good rooms they were. Instead, Lillan went into the spare room which was her bedroom now. Mama had hung some curtains there and had put a bright throw on the bed. But the room was still dark and small. It was a closet-like room. If it weren't for the window it would have been a closet. Lillan climbed on the radiator. From there she could see through the window beyond the rooftops that dropped down towards Mälaren. The chimneys and air vents looked like hooded hawks perched on the apartment roofs. Far away the gold crowns on the state house gleamed. Lillan looked out. It was a bright day out there, but her room was dark. She climbed down and went into her mother's room. On the side table along with the little china figurines that Mama loved was a picture of Lillan with Papa, but Mama had bent Papa's head around. Now it was a picture of Lillan smiling up at nobody.

She looked at herself—small, and dark, and thin, with big eyes and a big mouth. She had worn her hair in pigtails then. But now it was short and it had begun to curl a little. She was still thin, and her mouth was still too big.

Lillan removed the picture from the frame.

She bent Papa's head back and looked at him. He was laughing, but there were creases all across his face from the bending, as if someone had crossed his face out with white lines. Lillan took the picture and began to bend her own face back. That started to make creases, too. Lillan stopped. She felt uneasy. Mama had said that sometimes you had to give up loving somebody. She bent Papa's head back again the way Mama had had it. Slowly she put the picture back in the frame. Couldn't it just as easily be Lillan's part of the picture that was bent out of sight?

She bit her lip and turned away. Lillan went

to look at herself in the mirror. She looked the same as always only a little pale. Mama's purse was on the little birch dresser. It was open. Lillan looked inside. There was nothing much there. Then she saw the change purse. She opened it. There were several coins. Lillan hesitated a moment, then quickly she picked a copper five cent piece out and stuck it in her pocket.

Hurriedly she left the room. Down at the end of the hall she could still hear Mama talking. Quietly she took her sweater and went out, down the old marble staircase and out to the street.

The air was sharp and bright. Next door was the little grocery. Lillan took the coin from her pocket and ducked into the shop. There she bought a large caramel.

She had it in her mouth at once and ate it hurriedly, hardly tasting the sweetness, though it was the first in a very long time. Then she ran back to the apartment house and climbed the stairs. The old elevator was coming down. Maybe the lady had gone.

Lillan opened the door to her home softly.

"Oh there you are!" cried Mama. "Where did you go?"

Lillan swallowed, but her mother went on, not remembering her question. "She took it, Lillan! She took the rooms." And Mama caught Lillan in her arms and waltzed all around the oriental rug in the living room.

Lillan could hardly smile. The sweet taste in her mouth turned sour. She began to feel very sick, as the tapestry whirled strangely out of sight before her very eyes.

3

---

The tenant moved in a few days after that. It felt odd to know that someone strange was living and breathing in the same house, someone you didn't know at all. The lady was gone most of the day and came in only at night. Once Lillan peeped into the living room. She saw papers and books all over the Louis the Fourteenth sofa, and a suitcase was leaning up against the tapestry. Lillan winced and closed the door. She would never go in there again.

Mama was good as her word. She bought meat for one of their dinners that first week with a portion of the tenant's rent. She bought two oranges a few days later. They were hard and seedy and sour. Mama and Lillan were both disappointed, but it seemed right to Lillan. It seemed just that the living room money should buy sour oranges.

Mama was very careful with the tenant's rent. Every cent was spoken for.

"Tomorrow we're going to buy you new shoes, Lillan," she said one day that week. "School starts in two days. Aren't you glad, darling? You'll meet new friends now."

Lillan frowned. She thought it was her mother who would be glad of school starting. Then she could go to work. She didn't have to worry about Lillan anymore.

"You don't look a bit glad," said Mama and pinched her pale cheek. "You've looked so gloomy lately. I know it's been hard, darling. But starting again is hard. Why don't we buy your shoes today? Let's put on our best things and go."

Lillan looked at her mother and tried to smile.

"That's the first smile I've seen in a long time," said Mama happily.

And suddenly Lillan felt better. Mama had noticed. She went to her room and took off her clothes. She drew her organdy dress with the little yellow flowers from the closet. It was a summer dress, too thin for the cold air that was the sign of early autumn. But Lillan didn't care. Today felt like yellow flowers.

She went to her mother's room. Mama was almost dressed and while Lillan waited she tried not to look at the photograph among the china figurines on the side table. She didn't want anything to spoil their day.

Soon they were ready. They took the old elevator down and went out into the bright street.

"Let's walk," said Mama. "We can save the streetcar fare and maybe we can have a treat instead."

They hurried past Slussen with its clover leaf of traffic and the Katarina elevator. They went past the quay where the ferry left for Tivoli and the zoo at Grönalund. Lillan shut her eyes to the ferry. Papa used to take them on it on Sundays for excursions to Grönalund. He used to buy them ice cream cones with whipped cream. They used to sit in the open air restaurants and watch all the people. Lillan looked determinedly away from the ferry.

She and Mama walked past the castle and over the bridge through Kungsträdgarden to N.K., the big department store.

Soon Lillan found herself in the shoe department. For a moment she looked hopefully at the dainty party shoes in the case. There were only a few there, but Mama shook her head.

"No, darling, we have to get solid shoes, shoes that will last a long time."

Lillan tried on the heavy soled shoes. They were dreary and brown and useful. But Lillan saw how pleased Mama looked, and at last they settled on a pair with ribbed rubber soles and sturdy leather laces.

"Those will last," said Mama with satisfaction. Lillan tried to look pleased, but she noticed how her mother winced when the shoe salesman asked for forty crowns.

"So expensive," she murmured worriedly.

Lillan looked away. Her mother didn't want to spend the money. Lillan looked down at the new shoes on her feet. She didn't really want them now.

"I can use my old ones, Mama," said Lillan determinedly.

"Don't be silly," said Mama. "Of course, you need shoes. She'll wear them," said Mama to the shoe salesman.

Lillan blushed. There it was again that funny way of scolding. Only Lillan knew if her mother didn't have her, she needn't worry about money.

"Come on, darling, we have to get something else."

They went through depleted aisles of merchandise. The store looked a little empty. Lillan followed behind her mother silently. They stopped in the fabric department and her mother fingered some cloth thoughtfully. But then she straightened up and turned her back to the counter. On the first floor they came to the stationery department.

"Lillan, you look around a minute. I'll meet you at the front door," said Mama briskly.

Lillan looked up, a little bewildered.

"Go on now. You're a big girl. I'll soon be there," said Mama.

Slowly Lillan went down the aisles looking at things but not really seeing them. At Morfar's it had been like that for Mama, too. They had just gone on living but not seeing anything. They had just kept going. But now it was different. Now Mama was determined and brisk and busy. Now they were back in Stockholm. Now everything had to start new. But the other way seemed better. At least it didn't hurt. Lillan bit her lip.

She stood at a counter. There were little paring knives and household things. They looked dusty and forgotten. Lillan reached up and almost touched a spoon with a round handle. Nobody would miss it, she thought. She could put it in her pocket. She could take it. Nobody would know. Lillan bit her lip again. She looked around. She could just see Mama walking towards the main entrance. Lillan touched the spoon. Then a lady came to the counter.

"Is there anything you'd like, little girl?" said the lady.

Lillan blushed. "No. No, thank you." She turned and rushed away. She felt hot and ashamed. Mama was waiting for her. Would she notice?

"Good. There you are," said Mama and didn't look at her. Lillan felt relieved. Mama didn't notice. "Let's go and have a treat now," she said.

They went out in the nippy air. Mama found a milk bar close by and they sat down at a little table.

Lillan looked longingly at the pastries on the counter. But Mama turned to the waitress and ordered cocoa and coffee.

Lillan drank her cocoa. It was made with water and tasted a little bitter. Mama sipped the coffee slowly to make it last and she seemed

so pleased.

"I'm glad we got your shoes, Lillan," said Mama. "I'm glad we went out. It's so nice to see the stores and the people. Don't you think?"

Lillan nodded and looked into her empty cup.

"You know, I asked you to go off in the store for a special reason," said Mama.

Lillan looked up. Mama's brown hair fell forward over her face in a girlish way as she leaned over her purse.

"I wanted you to go away so I could buy you a surprise," Mama went on. "Here it is." She handed Lillan a flat brown parcel over the table.

Slowly Lillan took it. She didn't deserve a present.

"Open it!" cried Mama.

Nervously Lillan opened the parcel. Inside was a wooden pencil case with a painted lid and a metal clasp. It had pretty hearts and leaves in green and red. Lillan opened the case. There were pencils inside, new pencils and a sharpener, a little ruler and a big pink eraser.

"For school," said Mama. "Do you like it?"

"Oh yes, Mama," said Lillan. It was the prettiest thing she had seen in a long time. Lillan looked at Mama in bewilderment. "But it must have cost so much."

"It did," said Mama and wrinkled her nose. "We'll have to eat herring for a whole week," she said, "but it doesn't matter."

"It doesn't matter," thought Lillan and she felt a stab of guilt and happiness all mixed up.

She picked up the pink eraser. It was so smooth. It smelled so beautifully of newness and rubber. Lillan held it gently in her hand and thought about what school might bring.

# 4

Mama spent the next day lowering the hems on Lillan's dresses and fixing her own clothes. Mama's work would start soon. They both had an air of anticipation. Lillan looked at her pencil case many times and at the four dresses in the closet all ironed and ready. She couldn't help but feel excited.

The first day of school was only half a day. Pencil case in hand Lillan walked to school by herself. It wasn't far. She crossed the busy street by the apartment, went through the churchyard which was a little spooky, then up a long wooden staircase and a steep cobbled hill. And there was the school.

Inside the classroom everything smelled of newly waxed floors and desks, of washed black-

boards and disinfectant. Lillan looked around
her class. She saw two girls with shoes like her
own and she felt better about them. She put her
pencil case carefully on the desk and was
pleased to see her neighbor look at it approv-
ingly. The morning sped by quickly with the
passing out of books and the teacher's learning
of names. Her teacher called her Ingalill. It was
her real name, a little strange since Mama never
used it. But it was not unpleasant. Soon the
class was out and it was time to go home.

Lillan took her pencil case carefully in her
hand and went out. Her neighbor stopped her.

"You're Ingalill, aren't you?"

Lillan nodded.

"I like your pencil case," said the girl. She
was blond with long braids, and the teacher
had called her Britta.

"It's new," said Lillan. "Mama bought it for
school."

"I like it. See you tomorrow."

Lillan watched the blond girl head home.
She waved to a policeman who was stationed
near the school, and then she disappeared.

Lillan walked slowly down the cobblestones.
The policeman waved to her and she waved
back. Everyone seemed friendly. Mama was

right. She was glad school had begun. She was glad no one had a pencil case like hers.

When she came home Mama had lunch waiting; a boiled egg and anchovies and hard rye bread. She ate it all, though the anchovies stung her mouth with salt. And then Mama settled back and wanted to hear about school.

Lillan told her all about it. Mama seemed pleased though her mouth looked a little worried.

"Lillan," she began. "You know I won't be able to be home for lunch. You will have to take your lunch to school in a bag and eat it there. I've talked to the school and they have given permission."

Lillan frowned. She hadn't though of that. When all the children went home she would be by herself—a whole hour.

"Darling, it's the only way," said Mama and her brisk voice was back. "You won't need to stay inside the school, of course, unless you want to. As long as the weather is nice you can have picnics in the churchyard. There are benches there. Then you can look in the shop windows, too, if there's time."

Lillan looked down at the red and white tablecloth. Why was it that when things were nice there was always something . . . something to ruin it all?

Mama shook her head. "Don't make it harder for me, Lillan. I don't like it either but you have to be grown-up about this."

She rose and began clearing the dishes. Lillan didn't answer. What could she say anyway? It was all decided for her like everything else had been. Grown-ups just decided and that was that. Lillan sighed and went to her room and closed the door.

As the days went by Lillan began to dread the lunch hours. None of the children had said anything the first full day. They had all gone home. Only Britta had looked questioningly at Lillan when she made no move to get her coat.

Lillan had eaten her lunch quickly at her desk and the teacher had been there looking at her in a sympathetic sad sort of way.

Lillan busied herself with the pencil case so the teacher wouldn't look at her in that way. But it was no use. The teacher came over to her desk full of ready understanding and curiosity.

"That's a lovely pencil case, Ingalill," she had said. "Who gave it to you?"

"Mama," Lillan had murmured.

"She works, does she?"

Lillan nodded, closing her lips and staring at the pink freshness of the eraser.

"And your father, does he work, too?"

Why did she ask? Lillan felt resentful. Why did she need to know? But you couldn't be rude to a grown-up. You answered a teacher because you had to. Lillan felt weak with the anger she couldn't show.

"I don't have a father," said Lillan at last and glared at the desk. Slowly she was aware that the teacher was embarrassed. Lillan noticed how she shifted her feet. Then Lillan felt better.

"I'm sorry," the teacher said and had gone out of the room.

Lillan had remained a little longer. It was all so quiet. She was alone and felt as if she were forgotten among all the empty desks. She had begun to look in the desks then, lifting the lids gingerly, looking at what the other children had. But she had been afraid of the teacher returning so she had left and gone outside to hang on the chinning bar in the playground. She hung a long time suspended looking at a world turned upside down. That was the first day.

But Britta had cornered her a few days later

*33*

after school.

"Don't you go home for lunch?" she had asked.

"No." Lillan shook her head and looked at her thick school shoes.

"Why not?"

"My Mama works."

"Oh? You don't have a Papa then?"

"No," said Lillan. It wasn't exactly the truth. She had said the same thing to her teacher. Maybe Britta would stop asking questions the way her teacher had.

"Is he dead?" persisted Britta looking straight at her.

"No," Lillan had said finally and had turned and walked down the long cobblestone hill.

Now she was afraid that Britta would ask more, that other children would ask why she did not go home for lunch. In a way she wished they would. Then she needn't wait for them to ask. Lillan hung around the classroom during the endless lunch hours. Sometimes she went out and chatted with the policeman, who was friendly and never asked anything. But mostly she stayed inside, looking in the desks when the teacher wasn't there, and doodling on the blackboard.

Then one day she saw a pretty little bracelet left in a corner of Britta's desk. Lillan fingered it. She tried it on. It was the kind of present Papa might have given her—now that she was older. Slowly Lillan took it off. Carefully she put it back only she tucked it far behind a stack of papers. She wanted to hide it away from Britta and from herself, too. It had reminded her again. Everything reminded her that Papa didn't love them anymore: the lunch hours alone at the school, the closed door to the living room where someone else lived, Mama's busy briskness.

Lillan bit her lip and went to the blackboard. She drew huge angry faces all over the slate. They were ugly faces. Then she began writing furiously.

PAPA DOESN'T LOVE US. PAPA DOESN'T LOVE US.

Suddenly she was aware of someone looking at her through the glass door of the classroom. She spun around. Her teacher stood there with dismay all over her face. Lillan froze. She felt helpless. She stared back, only not seeing the teacher but the ugly faces she had drawn.

The teacher walked in. Carefully she put her hand on Lillan's shoulders.

"We'll have to erase all this," she said quietly. "The children will be back soon. I'll help you."

Lillan was relieved she didn't say more. She watched silently as the angry faces vanished with the teacher's quick strokes. Now there was just dusty blackboard left.

Lillan turned away. She ran into the coat-room, fetched her jacket and bolted past the children coming up the hill for the afternoon session. She ran as fast as she could down the cobbled hill, down the wooden staircase that echoed with her footfall, and into the church-yard.

# 5

---

The churchyard was very quiet. Lillan could
hear the dry leaves rustling along the pebble
paths. The church bell struck the hour, and a
baby cried in a carriage not far off. Lillan pulled
her coat around her and huddled on a park
bench. She didn't think about anything. She just
sat there looking now and then at the mother,
who was reading a paper next to the baby carriage. The church bell struck the half hour.
Someone walked on the path. She could hear
heavy footsteps. Lillan looked up. It was the
policeman. He stopped and smiled at her.

*"Hejsan,"* he said.

Lillan turned away.

"You were in a great hurry a moment ago,"
he remarked, pushing his cap back on his head.

"It's not such a good idea running pell-mell down the hill."

Lillan didn't say anything. The policeman sat down next to her on the bench.

"Feels good to sit," he said. "You kids don't think so though, eh?" He laughed. "Sitting all day at school. The grass is always greener on the other side of the fence."

He looked at Lillan now. "It's no good sitting too long. You'll catch cold," he remarked. "Then you'll miss a lot of learning."

Lillan pulled her coat around her. She was cold.

"Come on, let's walk," said the policeman and lifted Lillan up by her elbows.

Lillan shook her head.

"Oh, yes," laughed the policeman. "I get lonely. You keep me company."

Slowly Lillan followed then. The policeman twirled his stick lazily in the air and they made their way around the gravel paths of the church-yard. Then the policeman turned to the wooden staircase.

"Up we go," he said.

Lillan hesitated.

"You're going back to school," he said gently. "Can't miss that, you know."

Lillan hung back.

"They'll miss you for sure," he said. "Most likely they'll call home. You wouldn't want to worry anyone." He looked at her frowning slightly. "Your mother would be very anxious."

Lillan bit her lip.

The school would surely call her mother at work. Mama would be brisk with her and angry. And suddenly Lillan had a vision of the photo-graph in Mama's room, only this time the frame was empty. Lillan shuddered.

"Here we go," said the policeman, and took a firm but gentle grip on her left elbow.

*39*

A short time later Lillan found herself in her own desk. The children were bent over their work. The teacher smiled at her. It was the same room, but different. There was an air about the room. Now Lillan could see Britta steal a knowing look at her. And a boy down the aisle did it, too. Lillan blushed. What had the teacher said?

The work in front of her danced crazily before her eyes. She couldn't work. She just sat there.

Towards the end of school she saw Britta waving her hand anxiously at the teacher.

"What is it, Britta?"

"My bracelet is gone," said Britta primly. "Someone stole it."

Lillan sucked in her breath and blushed. She remembered the bracelet tucked way inside Britta's desk. Then she noticed that a few children were looking at her. They knew she was there at lunch time. She was the only one there at that time, and their eyes accused her. Now Britta turned towards her with the same look. Lillan turned away and stared at her desk.

"Have you looked carefully?" asked the teacher.

"It was here!" said Britta. "Before lunch it

was here."

The bell for the end of school rang. The children put away their things.

"Look again," said the teacher over the noise. "Why don't you have Ingalill help you? Sometimes two sets of eyes are better than one."

The classroom cleared. Only Britta and Lillan were left.

"All right, you look," said Britta.

Lillan slowly rose from her desk. Her hands trembled. She went to Britta's desk. Slowly she pulled everything out of it; books, pencils and then the stack of papers at the end. Abruptly the bracelet clattered on the bottom of the desk.

"Oh, you found it!" cried Britta and dove for the bracelet.

The teacher nodded. "It's not polite to accuse anyone of stealing," she remarked. And then smiling gently at the girls, she left.

Lillan stood still. Her arms hung loosely by her side. She felt she had to say something, but she couldn't bring herself to say that it was she who had hid the bracelet.

"Thanks a lot!" cried Britta. "My mother would kill me if I lost it."

"That's all right," mumbled Lillan.

The girls stood looking at one another. Then

Britta smiled sheepishly.

"I did think you took it. I'm sorry."

Lillan blushed. "I tried it on," she confessed. "I guess I didn't put it back where you had it. I shouldn't have gone into your desk . . . but there's nothing to do at lunch time." Lillan blurted out her words and turned away. She liked Britta, but she didn't want to see what the other girl thought of her now.

"Oh," said Britta a little huffily.

"I'm sorry," mumbled Lillan and went to get her coat.

"Wait," said Britta.

Lillan hung in the doorway.

Britta came up to her. "The teacher told us about you."

Lillan felt herself growing red at the hair roots. She was right. There had been something different about the classroom earlier.

"The teacher said we weren't to ask you lots of questions. She said you ate your lunch here because your Mama works and your Papa doesn't live with you."

"What else did she say?" asked Lillian nervously.

"Nothing. I think it would be kind of fun to eat at school. I'm going to ask my Mama if

*42*

she'll let me do it, too. Tomorrow maybe we could eat together."

Lillan nodded. She felt better. The teacher had not said anything about her rushing off. No one had said anything and she was sure her mother didn't know. Britta wasn't angry about the bracelet. Lillan felt a great relief. In fact, she felt almost happy.

"I hope Mama says yes," said Britta in the hall. "Or maybe you could eat your lunch at my house."

Lillan looked up in surprise.

"I'll ask her," said Britta firmly, and her yellow braids bobbed up and down.

When Mama came home from work she was a little flushed and gay. Absently she tossed her coat on a kitchen chair. She whistled while she boiled some water for the potato cakes they were having.

"How was school today?" she asked and reached for the onions.

Lillan looked at her mother. There was something new about her. She frowned, not knowing what it could be.

"Did you have a nice day?" asked Mama again, chopping up the onions for the potato cakes. The knife flew across the flat chopping block.

"Mmmm," answered Lillan and watched her mother. It had been an awful day, but a nice one at the end. She shut her mind to the pictures she had drawn and thought instead of Britta. She would have to ask if she might go home with Britta.

"Mama," began Lillan. "If someone invited me to have lunch at their house, could I . . . would you let me go, Mama?"

"Of course, darling," said Mama right away. "That would be lovely for you."

Lillan felt pleased. It would be lovely.

Then Mama looked at her. She seemed serious. "You'll need to bring your own lunch. Everything is so expensive just after a war. An extra person would be a strain."

Lillan nodded and then she looked away. She didn't feel as pleased as before. Mama was right, of course, but why was she always reminding her how expensive everything was? Lillan shivered. Was she an extra person . . . a strain, as Mama put it?

She didn't want to go on with the thought. "I was planning," mumbled Lillan hastily, "to take my lunch."

"Well, then, that's fine," said Mama and smiled. "If you run along and do your school work we can play flower lotto tonight."

"All right," said Lillan and went to her room

*45*

to do her work, but her mind was too full of questions and reminders of what had happened. She couldn't work very well.

Why was Mama so pleased, Lillan wondered. But she couldn't guess. Distantly she could hear the key in the front door. That was the tenant arriving. Lillan sighed. As long as they were by themselves in the apartment it didn't seem so bad not to use the living room. But when Lillan heard the tenant, she always winced. She tried not to think of it. She tried to think about playing flower lotto and about tomorrow. Maybe tomorrow Britta would have her lunch at school. Maybe she would go to Britta's house.

As it turned out Britta neither brought her lunch nor asked Lillan home. It was as if she had totally forgotten. Lillan didn't know what to think. She tried to feel as if she didn't care. But she did care, especially since Mama had seemed so preoccupied and pleased the night before. Of course, she had paid attention to Lillan and they had played more games than usual. But her mother wasn't fully there. Something lay in the air and Lillan couldn't share it. She wanted to ask what had pleased Mama so, but somehow she felt she shouldn't.

Another day went by. Lillan felt blue. Britta was nice to her, but that was all. Just waiting was no good. Lillan wanted to do something. Maybe if she were to invite Britta home for dinner things would change. But would Mama agree to it? They could have something ordinary like pea soup and pancakes. It needn't be too expensive. Lillan felt herself grow excited. Surely Mama wouldn't mind . . . this once. Britta could come tomorrow and then maybe . . .

Lillan waited anxiously for her mother to return from work. She wiped the kitchen table and straightened her room. She dusted in her mother's bedroom, being careful of each little china figure that Mama loved so. At last she heard the key in the door. Lillan ran to the hall.

"Hello, darling!" cried Mama.

Lillan stopped. Her mother looked so fresh and happy. And then Lillan noticed the rose on her mother's suit jacket. It had not been there in the morning.

"Come into the kitchen," said Mama.

Lillan trailed behind her down the hall. "Mama," said Lillan, "I'd like to ask someone for dinner, can I?"

Her mother didn't hear her right away. She

whistled gayly and brought down a glass from the shelf to put her flower in.

"Mama," said Lillan much too loud.

"Yes, yes, darling." Her mother turned around.

"Mama, can I invite my friend Britta for dinner tomorrow?"

"Oh darling, not tomorrow," said Mama. "I'm having company. We're having company. Someone nice. You'll like him."

Lillan froze. "Who?" she asked, feeling a little apprehensive.

"A man who works in my office," said Mama.

"His name is Jon Almkvist. He'd like to meet you."

"Did he give you the flower?" asked Lillan slowly. It began to dawn on her why Mama had looked so pleased the last few days. Lillan felt suddenly lost and afraid and terribly disappointed.

"We can have your friend another day, darling. It's just that I've already invited him."

Slowly Lillan rose from her chair and walked to her room. She closed the door firmly behind her. Then she scrambled up on the radiator and looked out across the gray waters of Mälaren. The smelt fishermen were out in their boats still. Their round nets hung suspended over their little green boats. Lillan looked but didn't really see. Her eyes filled with tears. Ever since Papa had left, so long ago now, she seemed not to have a place. Mama had been sad and distant at first, and then brisk and worried. She had tried, Lillan knew, to make things seem the same as always. But they weren't. They couldn't be. Too much had happened, and it seemed to Lillan that there wasn't room for her anywhere.

Now Mama was pleased and happy and further away than before. Lillan felt the tears come. She stood there a long time.

*49*

Lillan never wanted the next day to come. She lay awake a long time. Mama had found her crying on the radiator. She had tried to comfort her, to explain that Lillan could certainly have a friend home but not this particular night. She asked Lillan to be reasonable. After all, she, Mama, had not had anyone for dinner ever since . . . well, for a year at least.

"Next week," said Mama, "next week it's your turn. All right? You pick a night next week, and we won't have pea soup for your friend. We'll have something very nice."

Lillan had not dared do anything but calm down and appear to be reasonable. She had smiled a little trembly smile and had nodded her agreement. But she didn't mean it. She felt angry and afraid. Would Mama want her there when the man came for dinner? What would Lillan do? She shut her eyes tight and tried to sleep, but all she saw was Mama pleased and flushed with a rosebud in her suit jacket.

But the next day did come, as it had to. And Lillan set off for school as usual. The policeman waved to her. The sun was bright in the crackling cold day. Everything around her seemed so cheerful, not at all as she felt.

She trudged slowly up the cobbled hill and before the tardy bell rang she made it to her school desk. When she opened her desk to take out the pencil case she found a neatly folded little note in it. The teacher was taking the roll call and Lillan had enough time to read the note.

*Mama said I could stay for lunch! Isn't that good? Britta.*

All at once Lillan felt better. She looked over at Britta and nodded to her friend. The bright morning air that came through a crack in the windows seemed somehow to be right and the schoolwork lay waiting in a neat, almost appealing order. Perhaps the day would be much better than she had first thought. Perhaps she had been a little too hasty to think the worst. Slowly Lillan set to work and somehow the time flew by until the lunch bell rang.

This time it didn't matter that the others left for their homes. Britta was staying! The teacher smiled at them and said they could pull their desks closer if they wanted to. Then she left, too, and the girls were alone together.

Britta tossed her head and her long braids bobbed behind her. "You know," she said, "I thought I was never going to get to stay for lunch. I must have asked my Mama fifty times."

Lillan smiled. "I thought you'd forgotten."

"Oh, no," said Britta, "but grown-ups have a stupid habit of thinking of their grown-up things. They just forget or they think something is inconvenient. They always have something else planned. Have you noticed that?"

Lillan nodded. "I thought it was just my mother," she murmured.

"They all do it," said Britta as if she knew and as if she were a hundred years old. Lillan had to laugh.

"Don't laugh," said Britta with a mouthful of sandwich. "When was the last time you asked for something that was 'inconvenient?' "

"Yesterday," said Lillan and had to laugh again. "I asked my mother if you could come for dinner tonight."

"What did she say?"

Lillan hesitated. Should she tell Britta about her mother's friend?

"Well, she said fine, but not tonight. Another time."

"There, you see, I was right," said Britta and the satisfaction on her face was plain.

"She said you could come a night next week. How is Thursday? That is if you want to and your mother will let you?" Lillan waited expectantly.

"I'd love to," said Britta. "That gives me seven days to get an answer."

Then they both laughed and the lunch hour passed very quickly. In another few hours school was out and Lillan flew home. She felt so pleased that she wanted to do something for her mother. She tidied the kitchen and put away the clean breakfast dishes. She combed her hair and put on a fresh dress. Then she straightened the coats in the front hall closet.

When her Mama came, everything was in sparkling order. She noticed it immediately.

"You couldn't have done anything nicer," said Mama and picked her up and twirled her around the front hall. She planted a big kiss on Lillan's cheek. "You look wonderful, darling. Now we need to fix a delicious dinner."

Lillan felt so strangely happy. It was as if Mama were all with her, as if they were great conspirators together.

Soon Lillan was chopping onions and anchovies for the lion's eye that would be the first course with hard dry bread.

"Men love that," said Mama. "Then we'll have sjöman's biff and cucumber salad. Oh, it isn't the Grand Hotel, but it's satisfying."

She spread a lovely table cloth on the scarred

kitchen table. Then suddenly she stopped. Lillan looked up in surprise.

"You know," said Mama slowly, "this is the kind of time I really miss the living room."

Lillan looked away. So her mother missed it, too. Knowing that made a difference. Lillan felt suddenly warm inside. Then her mother did miss things, too, things that mattered. She wasn't all brisk and practical.

Lillan smiled slowly. "I know, Mama. But maybe, maybe we could decorate the kitchen. We could make it homier."

"What a lovely idea," said Mama. "Let's!"

And hurriedly they set about clearing everything away from the counters. They put colored paper around the lamp that hung down from the ceiling. They pulled in the easy chair from Mama's bedroom and put it in a corner. They fetched the radio and tuned in on some lovely music. Soon the kitchen was hardly recognizable.

"Let's keep it this way," said Lillan. "It looks . . . it looks like a home," she blurted out.

Mama looked at her seriously. "Yes, Lillan," she said. "I know. We haven't had it very homey. We'll do this often, but for every day it's not practical."

55

Lillan winced a little, but she knew Mama was right. What mattered was that it could be like this, and that it was like that now.

Then Mama went to freshen up and they were both ready.

At last the doorbell rang. Mama gave Lillan a quick smile and took her hand. "Come on, darling."

They both opened the door. There stood Jon Almkvist. Lillan drew back a little. Somehow he was not what she had expected. He was a very big man with brown hair and brown eyes. The hand that shook hers was so big her fingers disappeared in it completely.

"You must be Ingalill. I'm glad to meet you." His voice was that rumbling sort that seems to start from the heels. Lillan stared.

"Oh, dear," he laughed, "I must have scared you." The laugh seemed to bounce off the walls.

Lillan shook her head. There was just so much of him. Somehow she wasn't prepared. Papa was a slighter man, with quick agile gestures and long fingers. He had always worn fine woolen suits and shirts of a light silky material. This man was somehow rougher. His jacket was heavy tweed, and his eyes were so frank and teasing that Lillan felt confused.

"Come into our parlor," said Mama quickly and led the way to the kitchen.

Lillan followed them both. She felt a little awkward and that funny feeling of not belonging wanted to come back again. She shook her head to try and make it go away.

Mr. Almkvist exclaimed over the kitchen and Mama was pleased. She made him sit in the easy chair and then he didn't seem so huge anymore.

Lillan served him the lion's eye and watched in amazement how it disappeared in a twinkling on one piece of hard bread after the other.

"Lillan made it," said Mama.

"Did you? I hope you will make it again for me?" The man smiled at her and Lillan nodded as she knew she should. Somehow she couldn't help feeling a little pleased.

They sat around the kitchen table and had dinner and talked of this and that. Lillan listened mostly, but she felt that she could stay even past her bedtime. Mama seemed so light-hearted, and Mr. Almkvist told silly jokes and talked about fishing and long walks in the woods.

Papa never went for long walks. He liked to ride and he liked cities with people and restau-

57

rants and theater. He liked such different things. Slowly Lillan grew sleepy and then Mama said it was time for bed.

Lillan got ready and crawled in between the sheets. She didn't know if she liked her mother's friend. But he wasn't unpleasant and somehow he had made Mama hers again. Lillan fell into a deep sleep and a small smile flitted across her lips.

Things went along beautifully for a long time.
Christmas came and went. Lillan felt content.
School was going very well and she and Mama
planned little excursions on Saturday afternoons
and Sundays. They went to the palace when it
was open to the public. Once they even saw the
queen going by in a big black car. They went
to the old town and peeked in the little shops
that lined the narrow cobbled streets. Of course,
they couldn't buy anything, but it was fun even
so because Mama seemed to have a bubbly kind
of joy and fun about her. They kept that feeling
of being plotters together, of sharing silly things
like going to fancy restaurants and pretending
they would stay until the *maître de* came to seat
them. Then they would remember something

hurriedly and leave. Once they even sat in the lobby of the Grand Hotel and played cards for a while as if they were waiting for someone. Papa would have been shocked. You went to fancy places like that because you belonged there. You didn't playact. With Papa you spent money—a lot of money, but they had not spent a penny. Lillan loved it, and she and Mama always giggled as if they had pulled off a great stunt.

In that time Jon Almkvist came for dinner once a week and Britta had been to the house several times. They had played ball against the concrete wall in the dark courtyard of the apartment house. They had looked at the puppies in the pet shop around the corner. Lillan had visited Britta, too. They had baked cookies at her house, and played marbles in the churchyard. Somehow with a friend the churchyard wasn't half so spooky.

Lillan wished things could go on like this forever. But they didn't because Mama seemed to loose her carefree self. Oh, it didn't happen all at once, but Lillan noticed that she grew pensive at night as if she were mulling over something serious. And then the phone would ring. It was always Jon Almkvist and Mama always talked a long time. Lillan would wait and wait and wait in the kitchen to continue the flower lotto game or the book they were reading. But when Mama came back she was preoccupied. Lillan kept hoping she would change back, but she didn't. She stirred her cup of tea over and over again, though there wasn't a speck of sugar in it. Sugar was too expensive.

Lillan didn't know what to make of it. She felt confused and at a loss. She wished Mama would tell her what was on her mind. They weren't collaborators anymore, and Lillan's life seemed to be full of holes and ragged edges again.

Then one day Mama told her she was going out for dinner with Jon Almkvist the next night.

"I've arranged," continued Mama, "that our tenant will see to your dinner, Lillan, and have you in bed at the proper time. It will be all right, won't it?"

Lillan was dumbfounded. She hardly knew what to say. The news was too awful. Not to have Mama there at night was unthinkable.

"Darling, it's only for one night," said Mama in a reassuring voice. "Our tenant is really a very nice person."

But Lillan hardly knew the lady except to say

good morning or good night. She felt afraid . . . afraid because without Mama everything was empty at home.

"Oh, Mama!" said Lillan holding back the tears with all her might.

Then Mama grew brisk and determined. "Lillan, I haven't been out on a grown-up evening for a very long time. You must understand. It's important for me and it's not the end of the world for you."

But for Lillan it seemed that way. The whole next day went by like a nightmare. Lillan couldn't keep her mind on her schoolwork. The teacher had to speak to her twice. And when Mama came home from work she got busy getting dressed up in her prettiest dress of black silk, a dress that Papa had bought for her. She brushed her hair until it was sleek and shiny. Lillan watched everything but from a distance as if her Mama were miles away.

Soon Mama was gone—her arm in Jon Almkvist's arm and only the damp feel of a hasty kiss was left with Lillan. She would have cried that minute, only the tenant was watching her.

Lillan found herself pulled into the living room with all its jumble of papers. It wasn't the old familiar room at all. Lillan didn't want to be there. The lady's eyeglasses blinked at her meaninglessly and Lillan found herself in a corner of the Louis the Fourteenth sofa answering questions haphazardly, trying not to cry. Even touching the carved arm of the sofa was no comfort to her. She only wanted the night to be over, for the time to pass.

Somehow they ate dinner and cleaned up afterwards. The lady tried to be pleasant and Lillan tried to be polite. But it was all so awful. Lillan no longer felt like crying. She only felt cold and empty.

Then at last it was time for bed. She crawled between the sheets. The tenant said good night softly and turned off the lights. Lillan was alone. Then she did cry, but only a little because she felt too empty to cry. Lillan was restless. She wanted something but she didn't know what just then.

Lillan squirmed between her bed covers. She turned her pillow to the cold side. She sat up. At last she got out of bed and tip-toed to her mother's bedroom in the dark. She closed the door and snapped on the light. The room was full of her mother. Only her mother wasn't there. Lillan touched the little figurines on the bedside table. She touched the bedspread and the comb and brush on the dresser. The room made her feel lonelier than she had felt all day.

Then at once she knew what she wanted. She wanted something that belonged to her mother, anything at all. She didn't dare take a figurine. What else was there? Something her mother wouldn't notice.

She saw them then. In a little silver dish on the dresser lay two shining crowns. Lillan picked them up. She held them tightly in her hand. They gave her a kind of comfort. Holding the coins made her feel better, and she slipped back to her room in the dark once again. She hid the money in her drawer. Somehow, knowing it was there, Lillan felt comforted. She closed her eyes in a kind of relief and drew a deep breath. Soon after she was able to sleep.

The next morning at the breakfast table
Mama had a happy flush on her face.

"How was it, Lillan? Not as bad as you
thought, I'd guess."

Lillan looked down grumpily at the hot oatmeal in her bowl.

"Oh, my little pouter," said Mama and came
around the table and lifted Lillan's face to her.
"Let me look at you."

Lillan dodged her mother's eyes. Her lips
quivered.

"There, there," said Mama and stroked Lillan's hair. "Being a good mother is almost as
hard as being grown-up about things. I want to
thank you, though. I had such a lovely time,"
said Mama dreamily. "It's been so long since I

had that kind of a pleasant evening."

Lillan felt a stab of pain. Hadn't Mama enjoyed their excursions? Didn't Mama like being with her? Lillan's eyes began to blur over. That was it, Mama liked Jon better than she liked Lillan. Maybe Mama had given up loving her like she had Papa. Lillan felt the emptiness of the evening before flood over her. She shivered in her chair.

Then Mama looked at Lillan carefully. "What is it?" she asked. "Lillan, you look almost ill."

This time Lillan couldn't keep the tears back. They came streaming down.

Mama came over to her. "Lillan, Lillan," she murmured. "Why are you crying so?"

At first Lillan couldn't say anything. She didn't dare. But the hurt got the better of her.

"You don't like being with me," she accused. "You like him better."

"Oh dear," said Mama. "What a silly goose you are." Mama kissed Lillan's tear-streaked face. "I like him, yes, Lillan. That is true. But I love you terribly. You and I belong together and we have a lovely time. It's just that Mama needs to have a grown-up time once in a great while. Maybe you can't understand that now,

*67*

but you will when you are bigger."

Mama held her closely. Lillan's crying grew softer and then it stopped. She felt a little comforted. Her tears dried at last and left her face feeling taut and sticky. But deep inside there was still that little pit of doubt. Lillan tried to ignore it, tried to eat her breakfast and to think of school. Maybe Britta was staying for lunch today. Maybe she was invited there.

"We'll have to hurry," said Mama, "or we'll both be late." She stacked the dirty dishes in the sink and went to her bedroom to get ready for the day.

Lillan went to the bathroom to put cold water on her blotchy face. She stayed there a while until Mama called.

"Lillan!"

"Yes, Mama," answered Lillan from the bathroom.

"I had two crowns on the dresser. Have you seen them?"

Lillan froze. She had forgotten about the coins.

"Lillan." Her mother came to the bathroom. Hurriedly Lillan covered her face with the washcloth.

"I must have put the money somewhere. I

*68*

need it for the bus fare. Did you see it?"

"No," mumbled Lillan, feeling grateful that her face was not visible.

"That's so strange," said Mama and went out to look some more.

Lillan stood tensely in the bathroom listening to her mother searching about the apartment. What should she do? She couldn't tell her mother that she had taken the coins. Not now. How could she explain that it wasn't the money she wanted only . . . only . . . Lillan felt stiff. She knew her mother would be late for work if she walked. She had to get the money back to her somehow. She just had to.

Cautiously Lillan went to her room. Mama wasn't there. She dug in her bureau drawer with trembling fingers and fetched out the coins.

"Lillan!" her mother called.

Fear and that empty feeling came flooding over Lillan again. Would her mother understand? No. Lillan decided she wouldn't understand. But that didn't matter. She had to return the money or Mama would be late for work.

With the coins hidden in her hand Lillan went to the kitchen and took her lunch off the counter. Then she fetched her coat in the hall and put it on.

Mama came to the hall. She had a worried look on her face. Lillan gulped. She had to give the money back. She had to.

Lillan didn't look at her mother. "Here," she said putting the money in her mother's hand and looking at the floor all the while. "I took them," she blurted out and ran for the door.

"Lillan!" called Mama after her. "Lillan come back!"

But Lillan was already hurtling down the old marble steps. She didn't look back. Her mother's voice hurt as it followed her, but she dashed on, across the wide street into the churchyard and up the long wooden staircase.

# 10

Lillan couldn't bring herself to go home after school. She stayed behind when all the children left. Britta said goodbye to her but Lillan could hardly bring herself to answer. She stayed by her desk and rearranged everything in it. She cleaned the blackboard for the teacher. She straightened the desks. She picked up scraps from the floor.

"Ingalill, that's a wonderful help," said the teacher at last putting on her coat. "But it's time to go now, don't you think?"

Lillan hung back. She looked up at the teacher hopefully. "Isn't there something more I could do?" she asked.

Her teacher laughed. "Ingalill, you've done so much already. If I didn't know better, I'd think you didn't want to go home."

At that Lillan winced. Reluctantly she got her coat from the hall and went out to the schoolyard. The wind was blowing and the sky was gray and overcast. Lillan shivered. She struck off across the yard instead of down the hill.

The policeman waved to her. "Hey! Aren't you going the wrong way?" he called after her. Lillan shrugged.

"Off visiting, then?" asked the policeman coming closer.

Lillan ducked her head in answer and hurried away. She could feel the policeman's questioning eyes on her back, but she didn't care. She was not going home yet.

Lillan wandered along the cobbled back streets in the direction Britta took going home. She passed a dairy store with a long line of people waiting to buy the blue waterish milk that was sold now after the war. She came to a kiosk where a little lady, bundled up against the cold, was selling pastilles and sour candy. Lillan stood there a while gazing at the candy. But she had no money so she went on. The wind felt bitter now, and Lillan was chilled through. It had begun to turn dark. She went down the

street where Britta lived. She looked up at the apartment house. There was Britta's bedroom window. But Lillan couldn't see anyone moving behind the glass. Could she go to visit? Lillan hesitated. She was so cold, but she knew she had not been invited. Resolutely Lillan turned away from her friend's home and set her course down the hill that would eventually lead to her own street.

On a corner she saw a glass store. The windows looked dusty. The store seemed a little depressed. But the wind was whipping past Lillan now and she shivered visibly.

Quickly she pushed her way through the door. A bell tinkled and an old man with glasses looked up from the counter.

"Yes, young lady?" he said.

"I'm just looking," said Lillan hurriedly, the way Mama had done on their excursions to the old town.

"No harm in that," said the old man pleasantly and Lillan was free to poke around.

Everything seemed so dusty and forgotten. Lillan supposed people just didn't have money for pretty things these days—only practical useful things. She went into a corner of the store. It was warmer there. And then Lillan saw the little porcelain figurines tucked into a corner. Quickly she went over to them. They were made of the finest china, the kind that seems translucent and so delicate she would hardly dare touch them. There was a little boy playing a flute, a swan with a gracefully bent head, a girl picking flowers. And deep in the case was a figurine that Lillan couldn't take her eyes off. It was a tiny pink elephant with its trunk extended and its feet tucked under it. A little pink elephant asleep. It seemed surrounded by a serene pink glow of light. Lillan sucked in her breath. It was so beautiful. It was something Mama would dearly love.

Did she dare pick it up? No. Lillan might knock the other figurines over. She stood and stared a very long time. At last the man from the counter came over to her.

"Well," he asked. "What's caught your fancy?"

Lillan woke up then. "How much are those figurines?" she asked.

"They're expensive," said the man. "Anywhere from thirty crowns for the big ones to fifteen for that little elephant there. I don't think a young girl like you has that kind of money." He cocked his head questioningly at her.

Lillan looked down. "Oh," she said.

Then the man turned a kindly face towards her. "It's getting very late now. It's already dark. They'll be worried about you at home."

Lillan nodded. Slowly she went to the door casting a last look at the sleeping elephant. She did so want it. But the man was getting ready to close the shop so Lillan must go. She let herself out into the dark street. Bicycles, five abreast, came hurtling down the hill with people on their way home.

Mama would be home already. She would be very worried. Lillan knew she must go home and yet her feet seemed to drag behind her as she slowly headed into her own street. If only she could give her mother the little elephant, then maybe Mama wouldn't be angry with her. But Lillan had no fifteen crowns. There was nothing for it but to go home.

When Lillan came to her own apartment house, Mama was in the foyer peering worriedly up and down the street.

"Thank God," she said when she saw Lillan. "Oh darling, I was so worried."

Lillan could hardly look at her mother. She remembered all too well what had happened that morning.

77

"Come upstairs," said Mama. "You must be frozen."

Lillan was, but not so much outside as inside. Mama took off Lillan's coat and made her sit down to the supper table. Lillan couldn't eat. She was waiting . . . waiting for Mama to say something about the two crowns she had taken.

Mama looked at her closely. "Don't you want to eat?" she asked.

Lillan shook her head.

"Do you want to talk first, then?"

Lillan couldn't answer. She burst into tears. "I'm sorry, Mama. I shouldn't have . . ."

"No," said Mama seriously, "you shouldn't have taken the money. That was wrong. But you returned it. And I'm glad of that."

"I just wanted . . ." Oh, how could she explain that it wasn't the money she wanted only . . .

"Lillan, you must never take anything that doesn't belong to you for whatever reason. That's stealing. Will you promise me never, never to do it again?"

Lillan nodded tearfully.

"We'll forget this," said Mama. "But I hope you will never do such a thing again."

Lillan shuddered. Mama said they'd forget it. But would she really?

"I'm sorry," said Lillan looking up at Mama, searching her face .

"All right, darling. Eat up," said Mama. "You must be hungry."

Mama smiled at her. But would she really forget? Would she?

Lillan spooned some soup into her mouth, but somehow it had no taste at all.

# 11

A whole month went by. It was growing more springlike outside. The horse chestnut trees in the churchyard were budding and the wind, though still cold, had a silkiness about it, a promise of better things to come.

Mama never mentioned the money Lillan had taken. And though Lillan could not help remembering now and again, she tried to put it out of her mind.

School was going well. Lillan took pleasure in her work, and many of the children looked up to her. It had become fashionable now to stay for lunch at school, and Lillan found that it was not only Britta but two or three others who brought their lunch bags.

Everything seemed better. Britta and Lillan

got together often and Lillan found comfort in her friend who was so matter-of-fact and sure of herself. Britta always bobbed her braids and spoke out about what she felt.

"Mama is always so busy. I have to tell her to pay attention to me," or "When Mama and Papa have company I have to be there like a little angel. And then they give you that look that tells you to disappear like some sort of gas. It's not right. And I've said so."

Lillan marveled at Britta's outspokenness. "Did you really tell your Mama that?"

"Sure," said Britta.

"But didn't she . . . I mean weren't you afraid or anything?"

"No," said Britta. "Why should I?"

Lillan didn't answer. She thought about how many times Mama had looked at her lately in just the way Britta had described. It only happened when Jon Almkvist was there for dinner. Those were the times she wished she could speak out like Britta. Only she was afraid to because then Mama might be angry, might stop . . . Lillan didn't want to think of it.

"Do you really tell your Mama everything?" probed Lillan. "I mean, even when you've done something really bad?"

"Well," said Britta biting her determined little lips. "To tell you the truth, I tell Papa. He's more . . . well . . . he looks at things more for what they are without getting all excited and upset. Then he tells Mama. And everybody starts over again."

Lillan listened and marveled. She didn't have a Papa to talk to, not in that way. But Papa had never listened like that anyway. He was always wanting you to listen to him or do the things with him that he liked. Lillan sighed. Now she didn't even have him at all. Oh, if only, if only she could be sure that Mama would understand everything . . . anything. But maybe you needed a Papa like Britta had. Then Lillan couldn't help but think just a little bit about Jon Almkvist. Mama liked him very much. Perhaps he was like Britta's Papa. Only when he was at home for dinner, he paid much more attention to Mama than to Lillan. It had started after the night when Mama had gone out for dinner. Somehow Lillan couldn't help but feel left out no matter if Mama very often did try to include her. But Lillan knew she would never dare tell that to Mama outright.

After talking to Britta, Lillan would try to be more confident.

"Mama," she would ask, "is Jon Almkvist coming for dinner again?"

"Yes," Mama would answer, looking pleased. She would whistle and prepare dinner.

Watching Mama made all of Lillan's self-confidence ebb away.

"Why did you ask?"

"Nothing," Lillan would mumble and again she felt as if she could never, never dare say what she felt.

Time went on and it became more springlike outside. Soon it would be Mama's birthday. What could she give Mama? Lillan racked her brain. It had to be something special. Something Mama would really love . . . something that would make Mama take more notice. Maybe if the gift were really right, Mama would be so pleased that . . . that she would love Lillan more.

As the time grew closer, the birthday came to occupy Lillan's thoughts more and more. She had no money because Mama couldn't afford to give her an allowance. But if she had had an allowance she would have saved every penny for something really grand. But . . . Lillan's spirits sank. Without money what could she give? She had nothing, nothing at all to give.

Then Mama noticed that Lillan seemed worried and more withdrawn than usual.

"What is it, dear?" Mama asked one day when they were alone.

The question startled Lillan. She opened her mouth. She was about to tell Mama that she needed an allowance for something special. But what was the use? Mama would only wrinkle her nose and scold in that funny way. "Darling, you know we can't afford it." No. Lillan knew she couldn't say it. She didn't dare.

But Mama went on. "Tell me," she persisted softly. "You look so worried."

Lillan shook her head. "Nothing," she murmured.

Then the phone rang and when Mama went to answer it, Lillan went to her room to stand on the radiator. She looked out past the chimneys and thought about how she had wandered around the streets after school the last few days. She had looked at shops before she went home. She had seen things in the windows, things Mama would like. She had stopped by the glass store on Britta's street three times now. She had just been able to make out the little pink elephant in the dusty corner if she pressed her nose to the display window. That elephant! That was what she really wanted to give Mama. But it was fifteen crowns! Lillan sighed. Mama would love it so. It was such a pretty thing.

Lillian looked out over the housetops, over the blue water that winked at her in the early evening light.

Maybe . . . Lillan tensed. Maybe . . . maybe she could take it. The thought scared her, but Mama's birthday was only two days away. Lillan just had to do something. She was sure the man would never notice that it was gone. People didn't buy pretty things nowadays, only useful things. He would never sell it anyway. Slowly a resolve grew in Lillan. She would take it! After school tomorrow. Then she would have something to give, something Mama would really notice.

Lillan couldn't concentrate the next day. The time seemed to drag interminably. At last the school bell rang and the classrooms emptied. Lillan hung around the schoolyard until all her classmates had left. She didn't want anyone seeing her. At last even the schoolyard was empty.

Lillan drew a deep breath and began to walk in the direction of Britta's street. She took her time trying to gather courage as she went. Then at last she turned the corner and headed down the hill towards the glass shop. Her feet began dragging. She took a few more steps. There was the shop. Could she really do it? Lillan bit her lip. Somehow there was nothing else that she wanted to give Mama. Lillan looked up and down the street. She saw no one she knew and that was a relief. Lillan threw back her shoulders and pushed the door to the glass shop open.

There was someone inside besides herself. The man behind the counter was helping another customer. He nodded to Lillan in acknowledgement.

"Looking again?" he asked pleasantly.

Lillan nodded. She didn't dare speak. Her voice would surely give her away. The man wandered with the customer to a distant corner of the shop. Lillan slid into the corner where the little figurines were kept. There was the elephant looking as serene and lovely in its pink glow as ever. Lillan sucked in her breath. Yes, Mama must have it.

She glanced over her shoulder. The man and the customer were deep in conversation over a glass serving dish. This was her chance. Lillan reached quickly up and snatched the elephant in her hand, dropping it into her coat pocket.

Quickly she looked to see if anyone had noticed. No. The customer was still debating with the glass shop owner.

Lillan looked up at the shelf again. There was a little dustless space the shape of an elephant on the shelf. She winced. The man would see it. Again she looked back. The customer had moved away behind the partition where the cash register was kept. No one could see her. Now was her chance.

Quickly, carefully Lillan rearranged the other figurines to cover up the empty space. No one would know anything was missing now. She drew in a breath. She turned away from the display. The elephant felt as if it were burning a pink hole in her coat pocket. But she mustn't rush away. She mustn't act frightened. When she and Mama had been at the Grand Hotel they had acted natural, as if they belonged. She must act that way now. Lillan tried to make her face natural. She looked at a few more shelves. She went to another part of the shop. Then finally she let herself out of the shop walking slowly pretending that her skin didn't prickle, that her hands didn't feel clammy and wet.

Once outside and out of sight she ran. She ran as fast as her legs could carry her. The elephant felt like a hard lump in her pocket. It banged her thigh as she ran, each time giving a sting.

Lillan didn't stop until she was home. She rushed to her room and closed the door.

Slowly, still out of breath, she took the elephant out of her pocket. It looked so serene as if nothing whatever had happened to it, as if it would dream of pleasant things forever. Lillan held it a moment but it seemed to burn her hand. Her fingers trembled. She couldn't touch it anymore. Quickly she hid it in her bureau drawer behind her pajamas. She slammed the door shut and found herself shuddering from top to bottom as if the room were not warm and familiar but cold and strangely foreign.

# 12

The next day, the day of Mama's birthday, Lillan was full of worries. She did the work at school, yes, but with only half her mind. Uneasily, her thoughts strayed to the elephant asleep behind her pajamas. Wouldn't Mama wonder where she got it? Lillan shook the thought away as she had the night before. Luckily Mama had kept her busy then with preparations for the birthday dinner. Jon Almkvist was coming to help them celebrate. Lillan had not had time to think how she would give Mama her present. But now, between arithmetic problems, the worries kept popping out. What if Mama asked? What would Lillan say?

She bit her pencil. 129 divided by three . . . would Mama believe her if she said she found it? She *had* found it. That wasn't a lie, but . . . Lillan felt herself flushing over her division. She had stolen it. Surely Mama would guess. But maybe Mama would love it so much that she wouldn't ask, would only be happy and pleased. Lillan sighed. 134 divided by two. She'd hurry home, that's what she would do. She didn't need to decide anything now. She could make up her mind about everything later.

School seemed to drag to a close at last. Lillan was the first one out of the classroom. She flew down the hill, down the long staircase and through the churchyard.

Don't think now, she told herself. Wait . . . wait . . . till you're home.

But once at her own front door Lillan stopped. She felt almost afraid to go inside. Now she didn't have to wait anymore. Now she could decide. Reluctantly Lillan unlocked the front door. She shut it softly behind her. Slowly she went to her room without taking off her coat. She pulled the bureau drawer open. There it was, a gleaming translucent pink spot of color. Lillan took it out carefully. It was beautiful, the most beautiful thing Lillan could imagine. She wanted so much to give it to Mama. Lillan sat down on her bed uneasily, placing the elephant beside her. Somehow she couldn't touch it. She could hardly look at it.

The whole day's worries came flooding over her. Deep inside she knew that Mama would never believe her. No one would lose a beautiful thing like that. Mama would know she had stolen it. What had Mama said?

"Lillan, you must never take anything that doesn't belong to you . . . for whatever reason."

But what could she give Mama instead? She wanted so very much to give her something special, something Mama would really notice.

"Never take anything for whatever reason."

Lillan glanced at the elephant. And then she knew Mama would never love it. She would hate it. She would hate Lillan.

Suddenly Lillan couldn't bear the sight of the elephant. She hated it because Mama would hate it. She had to get rid of it quickly before Mama came home, before Mama knew what she had done.

Gingerly, trying not to look at the figurine, she slipped it in her pocket. She ran out the door, down the staircase and out to the street. If she hurried she'd have time enough to get home before Mama came.

The man at the glass shop was standing by

his door. He was locking up.

"Wait!" Lillan called.

"My, my," he said. "Back again. I'm afraid the shop will be closed this afternoon. I have to meet someone at the train station in half an hour."

Lillan's face fell. What would she do?

"Don't look so disappointed," said the man laughingly. "I'll be open tomorrow."

"Oh, please!" cried Lillan. "Could I just go in for a minute. Please!"

The man looked at her questioningly but Lillan didn't care. The elephant felt like a great dead weight in her pocket. She had to return it. She had to get rid of it.

"Please," she said and her voice seemed to crack like thin ice.

"Well, only a moment then. I can't imagine what's so special to a little youngster like you," he said with wonder. "Hurry up then and take a peek. I'll wait here."

Lillan gave him a thankful look and when he unlocked the door for her, she rushed in.

In a moment she was in the corner of the shop by the figurines. Was the man looking at her? Lillan threw a glance back. No. He was lighting a cigarette. In a flash the elephant was

*94*

where it had been as undisturbed as ever. Lillan felt the relief flood over her and suddenly she was weak, so weak she couldn't move.

"Come now," called the man from the door.

Slowly Lillan made her way to the door. Her fingers trembled. She was shaking inside her coat.

The man looked at her. "Is something wrong?" he asked. "You look almost sick."

Lillan stared down at the sidewalk. She shook her head.

The man hesitated. He was about to say something but then he looked at his watch. Behind her Lillan could hear the man locking up.

At last she found her voice. "Thank you," she told him almost in a whisper.

"Don't mention it," said the man absently. He was already on his way and Lillan faced homeward, though her legs felt like two brittle sticks.

# 13

When Lillan reached her home she saw a long slender florist box leaning up against the front door. Immediately she knew this was Mama's birthday gift from Jon Almkvist. Gingerly Lillan picked it up and brought it inside. The carton looked so expensive. She stood with it in the hall realizing, as she was holding the gift, that it was something Mama would surely notice. And she herself had nothing at all to give. She had counted on the elephant, but now . . . desolation came crowding in on her. She had nothing and Mama would be home any moment.

Lillan felt the tears under her eyelids. What could she make? What could she do? Frantically Lillan threw the florist box on a chair in the hall. She dashed to her room, coat and all. Lillan pulled out all her drawers, searching desperately. Nothing was there, not even fresh paper for a picture. The tears came pouring out. Lillan jerked everything out of her desk, spilling her small possessions on the floor. What was that in the corner? Lillan grabbed it. It was an old Christmas card with writing on it. It was the only thing she could find.

In one quick motion Lillan tore the written part away. A jagged edge now framed a dusty picture of a Christmas tree. She couldn't give Mama this. Lillan sat down in the midst of the jumbled room. The tears made everything seem to crowd together.

"Mama," sobbed Lillan. "Oh, Mama."

Suddenly Lillan stiffened. She heard voices, a key turning in the lock. Quickly Lillan tried to dry her tears. Mama had brought Jon Almkvist directly from work. She would have to do something.

Snatching a pencil and the dusty card, Lillan dashed to the bathroom. She locked the door and turned the water on full blast.

"Lillan!" she heard Mother calling. "Are you home, darling?"

"I'm here," answered Lillan, her voice only a little more audible than the rushing sound of water running.

"All right, dear."

Still wearing her coat, Lillan sat down on the closed toilet seat. She held the card between her hands. At first she couldn't do anything. Then slowly, balancing the card on her knees, she printed.

I LOVE YOU, MAMA. HAPPY BIRTHDAY.

The penciled letters looked slanted and awkward. Lillan tried to correct them, but they only became worse. She dropped the card in the sink where the water streamed across it. No. She couldn't give Mama that. It was too late, too late for anything. Lillan felt desolate, but she knew she couldn't stay in the bathroom forever.

Slowly, carefully with the water still splashing loudly, Lillan opened the bathroom door. She tiptoed into the hall. There she froze. She saw Mama in the kitchen. She was holding a bouquet of flowers and Jon Almkvist had his arms around her. They were kissing.

Lillan gasped without a sound. She stared blindly and then she whirled on her heels and flew out into the hall.

Somehow she got out into the street. She ran, not to the churchyard, but back of the apart-

ment house, past the pet shop, down the hundreds of steps that led to the back alleys along the water of Mälaren. She didn't stop until she was exhausted, until she stood on the edge of the quay looking at the early evening light come creeping dark and unavoidable from the East.

Lillan couldn't think. She didn't know how long she had stood there. The cold night wind came whining across the bay. Lillan pulled her coat tightly around her. She shut her eyes tightly against what she had remembered seeing. But the vision sprang into her mind. It was there, stark and new, over and over again. Now Lillan knew it. Mama loved Jon Almkvist. She had stopped loving Papa. Now she loved Jon Almkvist and she had stopped loving Lillan, too.

Lillan shuddered. Where could she go? The wind was so cold. Lillan huddled against her coat. Slowly she moved away from the water. She saw a dim-lit doorway. Lillan went towards it and sank to the doorsteps. Voices came from a distance and then the sound of footsteps. Lillan hardly heard them. She crept further into her coat.

Then she heard the voices again. They were calling.

"Lillan! Lillan!" It was her mother. The footsteps sounded not far away on the cobblestones.

Lillan jerked to her feet. She began running, running away from the voices.

"Lillan! Lillan!"

She ran blindly on. But heavier footsteps followed her. And suddenly she felt a strong arm catch her. She was trapped. Lillan looked up. It was Jon Almkvist.

"Let me go!" she yelled. "I hate you. I hate you!" She hit him in the chest.

Then Mama caught up to them.

"Lillan, dear, what is it?" said Mama, and tears stood out like spots of light on Mama's cheeks.

"I hate him!" cried Lillan. "You love him. You don't love me. You stopped loving Papa. Now you don't love me!"

Lillan could somehow hear her own voice breaking out of her, rising strangely out of her throat.

"Oh Lillan, dearest darling," said Mama.

Lillan trembled and then she felt herself sag. Jon Almkvist said something that rumbled over the cobblestones. Lillan found herself carried, held closely to a heavy tweed jacket.

She could hardly remember what happened next, except that she was at home. That Mama had undressed her and had put her in her own bed instead of Lillan's.

Slowly the tears subsided. Lillan opened her eyes. There was Mama. Her cheeks were streaked with tears, too.

"Darling, darling," Mama murmured. "My dearest, silly goose." Mama put her arms around her.

"Mama." Words came reaching out of Lillan. "I wanted to give you something . . . for your birthday. I wanted you to have something. But . . ." Lillan's voice trailed off.

"It doesn't matter," said Mama and kissed her. "I'm so thankful you're safe. I love you so very much, more than you can guess."

Lillan heard the words. Her head sang with them. It didn't matter. Not having a present didn't matter. Her mother loved her. But then the old worry came over her.

"But Papa? You stopped loving Papa?"

"Yes," said Mama softly. "But it takes two to love. When Papa stopped a long time ago, when he didn't want to try, then it was no use. It was like loving a dead thing. Can you understand?"

Lillan closed her eyes. This was part of a grown-up world. She didn't know if she could understand. She felt Mama's hand stroking her head. It was warm and comforting. This was her world. It was not dead. Lillan reached up to Mama's hand and held it.

"I love you," she said. "I love you, Mama."

"And I love you, darling."

They were silent then and Lillan, holding Mama's hand, felt a warm tiredness creep over her. Slowly her eyes closed and she slept.

# 14

When Lillan woke up the next morning she was still in Mama's bed. For a moment she didn't know where she was. It didn't trouble her because a deep comfortable sleepiness lay around her, warm as Mama's blanket. She looked around slowly, her eyes growing accustomed to a new morning, a new day.

Lillan sat up. At once she realized where she was, and all that had happened the night before came back. Quickly her eyes searched for the photograph on the side table next to Mama's bed. She saw herself there, a small smiling little girl. Lillan reached out and took the photograph in her hands. She gazed at herself. Something very important had happened, something she needed to think about.

Lillan held the photograph carefully. She knew very well that Papa's picture was behind hers. But that didn't matter anymore. That was over, and only the little girl was left. Lillan tried to smile as she had in the photograph making her mouth go up at the corners. She wrinkled her nose. Maybe that little girl was over, too. No. But she did feel she was someone new now. Not Lillan. Not Papa's little one. She was . . . what was she? Lillan frowned at her picture. She said her name, "Lillan." Then she tried her real name, "Ingalill . . . Ingalill." That's what her friends called her, what her teacher called her. It had always sounded strange, and yet . . . Lillan nodded. It had Lillan in it. Ingalill was Lillan, but not all together.

Then Mama came in. "Good morning," she said looking carefully at Lillan.

Lillan smiled. "I slept the whole night in your bed," she said.

Mama nodded. "I'm glad, darling. I'm glad you slept so well."

"Mama," Lillan looked seriously at her mother, "Last night . . . I'm sorry . . . I"

Mama shook her head. "Last night is over. It's a new day. We start fresh today, you and I."

Lillan nodded. Her thoughts were all so new.

She felt a little uneasy.

"Mama, do you think, do you think I should call myself Ingalill?"

"That's your name, darling. You must decide about that."

Lillan frowned. "Everyone calls me that at school. Only it feels so funny."

"Well," said Mama. "You think about it. We can try it out at home."

"Would you call me Ingalill, just for a while?"

"Yes, we'll both try it." Mama smiled. "Ingalill, it's time to get up or you'll be dreadfully late."

Lillan grinned. No, Ingalill grinned. "Mama, I love you," she said, and Mama touched her hair gently.

"I know."

Standing close to each other they were quiet a moment watching the sunlight dance across the bedroom.

"Hurry up now," said Mama finally. "It's late."

That night in the kitchen Mama and Lillan played flower lotto. It was warmer outside and the early evening air came flooding into the kitchen. All that mattered seemed to be right there around the red and white checkered table-cloth. Lillan watched the flowers gather on her lotto board. It was a gay bouquet of Swedish spring flowers: *gullvivor, blåsippor, förgät-mig-ejer, natt och dag.* She could almost smell them. She was placing daisies on her board when the phone rang. The sound seemed to come from far away like the sound of a drill boring into a hidden place. Lillan frowned.

Mama went to answer the phone.

"Lillan! I mean, Ingalill, it's for you!"

For her? Lillan rose slowly. She picked up the phone wonderingly.

"Hello?"

"Ingalill?"

She stiffened. It was the deep rumbling voice of Jon Almkvist.

"Ingalill?"

"Yes . . ."

"Hello, it's Jon Almkvist here."

She waited silently.

"I'd like you to come with me to Grönalund tomorrow."

Lillan looked at the phone almost holding it away from her. She remembered how she had hit him. What had she said? "I hate you! I hate you!" Lillan winced. She couldn't give an answer. The silence seemed to go on endlessly along the telephone wires.

"Ingalill, are you there?"

"Yes," mumbled Lillan.

"You could bring a friend if you'd like to."

Still Lillan could not answer. She could hear Jon Almkvist breathing far away on the other side of the line. It was a soft expectant rumble of wind.

"Well," he said at last. "You'd better not make up your mind just now. Have a talk with Mama, then you can call me back when you've decided. Goodbye, Ingalill."

The phone went dead. Lillan held it a moment longer. It was a relief to hear the empty mechanical buzz of the telephone. She couldn't go with him, not after last night. She just couldn't.

"Ingalill," Mama came into the bedroom.

Quickly Lillan replaced the receiver.

"Who was it, dear?"

"Jon Almkvist," murmured Lillan.

"Oh?" Mama looked at her searchingly. "What did he want?"

"Oh, Mama."

"What, darling?"

Lillan slumped down on the bed. The old fears came back. Could she tell Mama? Would Mama understand? Lillan looked up. Mama was waiting. A look of concern crossed her eyes. Lillan looked away. Her eyes rested on the photograph. She saw herself there again. No, but that wasn't her real self anymore. That little girl was Lillan, a smiling frightened little girl. Suddenly she turned away from the photograph.

"He wanted me to come with him tomorrow to Grönalund," blurted Lillan, trying to make her voice steady. "I'm afraid, Mama. I said such awful things to him."

Mama smiled. "You don't have to go," she

said gently. "He would like you to, but he would understand."

Lillan looked up in surprise. "You mean you don't mind if I don't?"

"Of course not," said Mama.

Then a safe comfortable silence fell between them. Lillan sighed. Maybe it would be fun. She hadn't been to Grönalund since . . . since Papa had taken her.

"He said I could bring a friend," began Lillan, exploring how she felt.

"Fine. Maybe Britta would like to go. That is if . . ."

"Then he isn't angry about, about everything?"

Mama laughed. "Would he ask you to go if he were angry?"

Lillan couldn't help smile at herself. She hadn't thought of that.

She bit her lip. "Well, if Britta wants to go," said Lillan, "then I'll go."

"Fine," said Mama. "You'd better call and find out."

She closed the door softly and Lillan was left alone by the telephone.

# 15

Britta said she would love to go, and the next day the girls were ready and waiting, dressed in their best things. Lillan felt nervous, but Britta bobbed her braids and announced she wanted to go to the Tivoli on the roller coaster and the ferris wheel and into the fun house.

When Jon Almkvist did come they got all ready to start off. Mama gave Lillan a kiss.

"Don't be away too long, now," she said. "Have a lovely time."

Lillan nodded and they all said goodbye.

Towards Slussen they went, past the buses, the street cars and the Katerina elevator. It was a lovely crisp spring day. Britta kept up a constant prattle about all the things she liked at Grönalund, but Lillan walked silently beside

*111*

Jon Almkvist trying to keep up with his long stride.

Soon they found themselves on the quay. Not far off the ferry boat was churning its way across the bay towards them. The gulls whirled and shrieked in the clear sky. Lillan saw two quarreling over scraps. She tried to remember the last time she had gone on the ferry to Grönalund. Papa had been impatient with her for wanting to be up at the prow watching the water welter in front of the ferry. He had said it was more ladylike to sit inside.

Slowly Lillan woke up as the ferry groaned against the padded quay. Jon Almkvist put their tokens in the turnstile and they filed on board. Automatically Lillan made her way towards a seat.

Jon Almkvist put his hand on her shoulders. "Ingalill, don't you want to go up front?" he asked.

She looked up in surprise. "Is it all right?" she asked.

"Is it all right?" said Jon Almkvist heartily. "It's the only place on a ferry boat."

Lillan smiled and readily followed him and Britta to the prow. They stood up against the ropes as the ferry churned backwards. Salt spray was caught by the wind and spattered their faces. Lillan laughed. She dangled her arms down trying to catch more spray. The ferry swayed forward across the bay, past the Af Chapman and the military installation. Up ahead the hills of the roller coaster humped into view.

Lillan found herself bursting with excitement. How could Britta keep talking, talking? Couldn't she be quiet just a little while and just feel the rumble of the motor and the lovely swaying of the ferry? Lillan stole a look up at Jon Almkvist. He, too, was silent, listening only a little to Britta. Quickly Lillan looked away. She didn't hate him. Maybe she liked him. But she wasn't sure she wanted to.

Soon they were streaming out of the ferry with the other passengers up the hill towards Grönalund.

Papa always took them to Grönalund itself. He didn't like the Tivoli very much. It was too noisy and the wheezy waltzes of the merry-go-round gave him a headache. Lillan looked away from the Tivoli entrance. She wanted to go there as much as Britta, but she didn't want to say so.

Jon Almkvist hesitated. "Have you got a good stomach, Ingalill?" he asked.

Lillan nodded. Why did he ask?

"How about a quick ride on the roller coaster?"

Both girls smiled. Oh, yes, they assured him, they both had very good stomachs.

They hurried inside the gate of the Tivoli. Lillan watched Jon Almkvist pay for the tickets. Three?

"Are you going, too?" asked Lillan in amazement.

"When I'm here alone I can't go riding by myself. It looks too silly," said Jon Almkvist seriously. "You two are my excuse."

Britta and Lillan exchanged glances and then eagerly they clamored aboard a little car. Jon Almkvist sat between them. Up, up it chugged. Lillan clutched the metal handlebar. Up, up. Now she could see the bay. She could see the steel structure of the roller coaster below her. Then they were flying down the mountainous hill, shrieking. Only Jon Almkvist's voice was a deep roar compared to theirs. Around hairpin turns they went. Lillan cried out in alarm and immediately she found Jon's arm around her. It was like another strong handlebar. She felt embarrassed, but she didn't move away. She could see Britta's braids out of the corner of her eye, flying out behind her like two kite tails. What did Britta think? Lillan saw she wasn't paying attention. Then Lillan relaxed and after another three turns the little car slowed to a stop to let them out. They stood still a moment getting their bearings.

"Let's go to the fun house, please!" cried Britta.

Jon Almkvist looked at Lillan. "Do you want to?"

Lillan nodded. So they went. In the dark Jon took Lillan by the hand. His hand was so large she could put her whole fist in it and still have room left over. There were cold and hot blasts of air, moving floors and strange noises. Lillan shivered and tingled. She was glad of Jon's hand. At last they came to the end of the fun house where a magic carpet waited.

Lillan saw people sitting down and then all of a sudden they disappeared through a flap in the wall—whoosh, out of sight. She felt a little uneasy. She watched Britta fly through the trap door out of sight. It was her turn now. Lillan hung back.

"Come, Ingalill," said Jon softly. "We'll do it together."

She found herself pulled to Jon's lap and then

*115*

she closed her eyes. The trap door opened. A cold blast of air fell sharply against her face. They were falling, sliding in a tunnel of darkness. She clung to Jon's long legs. The blackness whined past her. At last the carpet slid to a stop in broad daylight and they were out of the fun house.

"Let's go on the ferris wheel!" cried Britta eagerly.

Jon disentangled himself and stood up.

"I think Ingalill has had enough," he said firmly.

Britta looked disappointed, but Lillan was relieved. It had been fun, but she didn't want any more.

"Just the ferris wheel," begged Britta.

Jon shook his head. "Not now. Let's go to Grönalund and watch the seals. Besides," he laughed, "I'm not made of money."

That settled it and Lillan felt pleased. They went up the broad street to the iron gates of the zoo. The air had warmed up and the girls no longer needed their sweaters. Jon carried the sweaters on his arm as they passed the cages one by one. A seal barked and a balloon man wandered past with a gay bouquet of colored spheres. Britta kept dashing ahead, shouting for them to follow. In a funny way Lillan wished she were not along. It would be so nice to just wander slowly, and not to say too much. She wanted to enjoy everything. It had been so long since she had felt a real party air. And there was a party air, despite the fact that people every day had to clip their food coupons, had to watch what they bought the way Mama did. It felt so strange and wonderful just to be having fun in the new spring air.

At lunch time they had long sausages with Slotts mustard on a tiny crusty roll. They walked past the ancient farmhouses of the outdoor museum and at last they flopped down on a sun-baked ledge.

Jon Almkvist sprawled out on the rock. Lillan felt tired and sleepy. She wanted to watch the clouds float by in the crisp sky. She just wanted to be. But Britta dashed up.

"Come on," she said. "I see something."

"I don't want to," said Lillan and was surprised how firm her voice was. "I just want to sit."

Britta looked at her friend in astonishment. She opened her mouth and then closed it. "All right," she said finally and sat down.

But soon she couldn't contain herself and up

she went to explore the woods behind the ledge.

Lillan was content to lie very still on the rock. She didn't want to move. With Papa they would have sat at an outdoor restaurant watching people and talking about them and the things Papa wanted to talk about. But Lillan just wanted to watch the clouds as they passed slowly and majestically.

"It's nice, isn't it?" said Jon, slowly stirring.

Lillan murmured her yes.

It was nice, nicer than she could have dreamed.

Too soon Britta came back and it was time to go. They wandered back to the quay and caught the ferry home again. Lillan and Jon took Britta up to her apartment.

When they were out on the street once again, Lillan sighed. She didn't want the day to be over. Jon must have felt the same way because he stopped in the street.

"I have an idea. Let's get your mother a surprise since she wasn't along. Shall we?"

Lillan smiled. "Yes," she said. Then her face fell. "I haven't any money."

"I do, though," said Jon, "a little. We'll pick it out together. Let's see, where shall we go?"

They went down the hill on Britta's street. All

at once Jon Almkvist saw the glass shop. He stopped.

"Let's go in here."

Lillan felt suddenly apprehensive. She hung back, but when Jon didn't notice and went right in, she followed slowly. He wandered around the dusty display cases.

*"Hej,"* said the man behind the counter when Lillan came in. "The figurines are still all there. You know where they are."

Lillan blushed. She wanted to leave right then.

"What figurines?" said Jon. "Show me."

Slowly, reluctantly, Lillan went to the familiar corner. She tried to shut her eyes to the elephant she knew would be there.

Then, as from a distance, she saw Jon pick it up from the shelf.

"I wonder if your mother would like this one?" he asked. "It's the prettiest by far. Do you like it, Ingalill? Shall we get this one?"

Lillan froze. The glass shop whirled around her. "No." She shook her head desperately. "No," she whispered and spun around. She dashed for the door.

"Wait!" called Jon after her.

But Lillan flew out to the street. In a moment

she was down at the corner, but Jon Almkvist came up behind her.

"Ingalill," he said. "What is it?"

Despite herself the tears began pouring down Lillan's cheeks.

"Come," he said fetching up her hand. "Let's go somewhere and talk." He took her along down her own street up towards the churchyard. Unwillingly Lillan found herself sitting on a park bench, feeling cold and miserable.

"What is it?" said Jon. "What's wrong? Don't you like the elephant?"

"Oh, yes," said Lillan. "It's just . . . we just can't give that to Mama."

"Why not?"

"Because." Lillan's lip trembled. Could she really tell him? She wanted to tell him. She wanted to tell someone. Lillan burst into tears again. "Because . . . I stole it."

"Stole it?" said Jon. "But it was right on the shelf."

"I know," said Lillan. "I put it back." How could she make him understand? "I stole it for Mama's birthday," she said and slowly she began telling the whole story. It poured out of her as if her small person was too small to contain it anymore.

Jon didn't say anything. He only nodded his head and listened.

At last Lillan stopped. She felt tired and empty.

"Well, Ingalill," said Jon. "That was a lot for a young girl to carry around inside. I'm glad you told me. We'll sit here a minute and then we'll go and buy the elephant."

"But . . ."

"We'll keep it a secret," he said gently. "Your Mama won't know she's getting two presents in one."

Lillan looked up in confusion. "I don't understand," she said and wiped her nose.

"Taking it was wrong. You know that. But when you took it back you did something that would have made your mother happy. That's what presents are . . . gifts that make people happy. But she won't know about it. We'll keep it our secret."

Lillan looked up in wonder. Jon was smiling at her gently, kindly. She couldn't smile back. She couldn't say anything. It was all so strange. But when Jon held out his hand towards her, she took it silently.

# 16

The day ended wonderfully. Mama was so pleased about the elephant she let out a gasp of pleasure.

"Oh, how adorable! How did you know I would love this?" She looked from one to the other.

Lillan couldn't quite look Mama in the eyes. She had wanted Mama to have the pink elephant so much. And now she had it. It was cradled in Mama's hand as if it always belonged there.

"It's the nicest figurine I've ever seen," said Mama caressingly.

"Ingalill picked it," said Jon.

"Did you? How wonderful. Thank you! And thank you, too, Jon."

Lillan felt a warmth creep up her cheeks.

Mama was happy, as happy as Lillan had ever seen her. She gave them both a big hug and somehow it didn't seem strange that Mama threw her arms around Jon.

"Let's have supper. I've made *Jansson's Frestelse* and *rull tarta.*"

"A sausage for lunch wasn't enough for me," confessed Jon. "Let's go."

They ate around the kitchen table. Mama even had a candle and then they sang old Folk songs.

Lillan's cheeks seemed to burn with pleasure. And now she began to look at the little elephant as it lay dreaming in the center of the table. It had a secret. The same secret she and Jon had. Lillan looked at it squarely. It wouldn't tell the secret and then she knew that Jon would never tell it either. Lillan sighed. How strange and new she felt. She belonged here with Mama, not in the living room, but around the kitchen table where the elephant lay and where Jon sat just next to her. Lillan closed her eyes. The refrain of a song rang out:

> Kom liljor och akvileja
> Kom rosor och salivia
> Kom ljuva krusmynta

Spring came then in all its glory. The trees burst into leaves. The birds sang in the churchyard. School was drawing to a close. Soon Lillan would be eleven years old.

She was excited about her birthday. Mama had said she could have four friends for dinner. Britta was one, of course. And the others were all the girls who now brought their lunches to school regularly. Mama said that, if Lillan didn't mind, they could eat porridge and fish pudding for two weeks and then there would be enough money to buy the cheapest tickets for *Tom Sawyer* at the Kungliga Dramaten. Of course, Lillan didn't mind. She had never been there. The big theater loomed like a giant adventure in her mind.

The two weeks rushed by and though Lillan screwed her nose up at the hot porridge, she didn't say a word of complaint. To go to the theater was something so grand, so grown-up, that it was worth all the porridge and fish pudding in the world. Going to the theater was something Ingalill would do, something the little girl in the photograph could never do. And Mama knew it. They planned it together.

The day before Lillan's birthday came, Mama had said she would be home late because she would stop to get the theater tickets after work for Lillan's friends, for Lillan and Mama, and even for Jon.

Lillan took her time going home. The world was so full of newness that she had to walk almost reverently. At last she found herself in the old elevator of her apartment house. Lillan got off at her floor.

What was that against her door?

Lillan dropped down to pick it up. It was a package but with no return address. The stamps on it were foreign. Lillan looked the parcel over carefully. The label was typed and it was addressed to her. Should she wait until tomorrow? Lillan hesitated. She let herself into the apartment. She could hear the tenant stirring in the living room. But somehow lately it didn't matter at all. Lillan made her way to the kitchen carrying the package carefully. She took her coat off and sat down.

Tomorrow would be so full of adventures. If she opened the package now it wouldn't matter. Lillan undid the twine. The brown paper fell away. A little note was there. Lillan opened it.

*127*

## Happy Birthday, Lillan,
### My Little One

Lillan stared. Her hands felt clammy. A package from Papa! It was the first thing she had heard in such a long time. But why was there no return address on the wrapping paper?

Slowly with trembling fingers, Lillan took off the tissue paper surrounding the gift. The unseeing face of a little baby doll lay there before her. Lillan stared. She couldn't understand the gift. Didn't Papa know she didn't play with dolls anymore? Didn't Papa know about growing up?

Lillan felt disappointed and a little angry. She glared at the doll's closed eyes. Then slowly Lillan softened. She began to understand. Papa had remembered. In his own way he had remembered her. Only to him she was his little one, the little girl in the photograph. To him she would always be that. And that was something. Lillan's eyes grew wet.

"Thank you, Papa," she said solemnly. "Thank you for remembering."

Then slowly Lillan wrapped the doll up again. Someday she would tell Mama about it. But now she secured the twine around the brown wrapping paper. Carefully she took the package to her room. Where could she put it? Lillan looked around. Then at last she knew the place for it. Deep inside the closet and out of sight she put it, closing the door to the closet as if she closed the door to an old and forgotten room.

# 17

Lillan's birthday was on a Friday, a sparkling late spring day. When she came home from school she found a big sign on the closed kitchen door.

HAPPY BIRTHDAY
DO NOT ENTER

Lillan looked at it. How could she contain herself until Mama came home? Impatiently she went to her room and shed her school clothes. Her party dress lay ready on a chair. Lillan reached for it. No. She must not be impatient. She must do everything slowly. Otherwise the time would drag forever.

Lillan went to the bathroom. She washed her hands and face. She combed her hair and tied a ribbon in it. Slowly she dressed taking care not to wrinkle the dress.

Wasn't it time yet for Mama to come?

Lillan glanced into Mama's bedroom. The alarm clock showed her there was still a half hour to wait. Lillan sat down on the bed. She sat there a long time trying to be calm, but there was a glowing excitement in her like a small burning brazier.

Wasn't it time yet?

Lillan jumped up and went to the front door. Distantly she heard the old elevator rumble. That must be Mama.

Lillan flew to her room. Once in her room she tried to compose herself. She was eleven. Today she was eleven and she must be more grown-up. It wouldn't do to be hanging out the front door waiting.

There was the key in the lock at last!

"Hello!" cried Mama.

Lillan smiled. Deliberately she composed herself.

"Hello, Mama."

"Where's the birthday child?" That was Jon Almkvist's deep rumble.

Lillan was surprised. He must have come with Mama directly from work.

"Where are you?" demanded Jon and the real sound of impatience in his voice somehow pleased Lillan.

"Here I am," said Lillan striding as calmly as she could out of her room.

"How beautiful you look. But how can you be so calm?" grumbled Jon. "I'm dying to open that door."

"You didn't open it, did you?" asked Mama quickly.

Lillan tossed her head. "Of course not."

"Well, it's time then. Go on, Lillan."

Mama quickly shed her light coat as Lillan slowly turned the handle. She stopped dead.

"Oh!" she said with delight. The kitchen was rearranged as for special occasions. It was cozy and warm. The easy chair was in a corner. The counters were cleared. On the table a single rose, candles and a cake stood invitingly on a lovely tablecloth.

"Oh, Mama, when did you do this? It wasn't here this morning."

"Well," Mama confessed, "Jon and I took a long lunch hour. We did it together."

Lillan looked up at Jon. She gazed at him wonderingly.

"Don't look at me like that," he laughed. "It's

not fair for ladies to be the only ones to plan surprises. Men need to have a chance at it, too."

Lillan smiled at him. "Thank you," she said, and turning to Mama she stretched out her arms. "Thank you, Mama."

"Wait," said Mama. "There's more." She nodded to Jon and Lillan saw him dig in his pocket. Out of his rough tweed jacket came a slender box wrapped in pink tissue paper.

"For you," said Jon, "from your Mama and me."

He pushed the present into her hand. Lillan held it gingerly. Quickly she looked at them both and then hurriedly she took the paper off. The box was open. Inside lay a young lady's, slender, beautiful gold bracelet.

"Oh!" Lillan sucked in her breath. "Oh, how lovely." It was lovelier by far than Britta's bracelet. But how could Mama have afforded it? How had she and Jon known that Lillan wanted one? She had never said so, not even to herself since that day at school long ago.

"Try it on," urged Mama.

Lillan was quick to oblige. She slipped it on and then she saw the little attached medallion that had been hidden before. It had writing on it. Lillan read it.

INGALILL it said in small neat letters. Lillan stood still a moment. It was so pretty she hardly dared believe it was hers. Then she flung her arms around Mama.

"Thank you. Thank you."

There stood Jon grinning behind his pipe. It seemed the only right thing, so Lillan flung her arms around him, too.

"Thank you," she said.

"Enough, enough," rumbled Jon gently. "Let's have tea before the girls come."

So they did, gathering around the table. Lillan touched her bracelet from time to time and sipped the warm, sweet tea.

Then Jon cleared his throat. "A toast," he announced, raising his cup.

> My heart feels so wide
> I have to confide
> I think I've caught her
> A grown-up daughter
> Happy Birthday!

Lillan blushed. What did he mean? She looked questioningly at Mama.

"Ingalill, Jon wants me to marry him," she explained softly. "He wants us to be his family."

"Oh," said Lillan in confusion.

Then Jon reached out a large hand and covered hers.

"Not right away," he said slowly. "When we are ready, Ingalill. All of us."

Lillan was speechless. She didn't know what to think. She could feel Jon's big hand over hers. It was warm and strangely light.

Slowly she glanced at Mama. Her eyes were searching for Lillan's, too. They were calm and certain. "When we are all ready," they seemed to say.

Lillan glanced down. Then slowly, seriously she nodded.

"Well," said Jon, "aren't there some girls coming soon? Don't we have things to do?"

Of course, in the excitement she had forgotten. Her friends were coming and then there was Kungliga Dramaten and *Tom Sawyer*. Ingalill stood up. Before her was a wonderful evening, the start of a whole new year. She looked from Mama to Jon, and she smiled. She knew it was a start for them, too, for all three of them.

# GLOSSARY

| | |
|---|---|
| *blåsippor* | liver worts |
| *crown* | unit of Swedish money worth about twenty cents |
| *förgät mig ejer* | forget-me-nots |
| *gullvivor* | cowslips |
| *Hej!* | Hi! |
| *Hejsan!* | Hi there! |
| *Jansson's Frestelse* | casserole made of anchovies and potatoes |
| *Kungliga Dramaten* | Royal theater, owned by the state |
| *Kungsträdgården* | King's Park |
| *lion's eye* | mixture of anchovies and onions eaten on rye bread |
| *Morfar* | Grandfather |
| *natt och dag* | pansies |
| *rull tårta* | jelly roll |
| *sjöman's biff* | a meat and potato casserole |
| *Slussen* | traffic circle in southern Stockholm |
| *Statshuset* | the Statehouse |
| *Tivoli* | an amusement park in Stockholm |

## *Translation of Song on pages 125-6*

Come lilies and columbine,
Come roses and garden sage
Come sweet balm-mint
Come heart's delight